H.Brown   GVCA

S0-BTE-677

Don't Tell the Whole World!

by Joanna Cole   illustrated by Kate Duke

HarperTrophy
A Division of HarperCollins*Publishers*

Don't Tell the Whole World!
Text copyright © 1990 by Joanna Cole
Illustrations copyright © 1990 by Kate Duke
Printed in the U.S.A. All rights reserved.
Typography by Patricia Tobin

Library of Congress Cataloging-in-Publication Data
Cole, Joanna.
 Don't tell the whole world! / by Joanna Cole ; illustrated by Kate
Duke.
   p.   cm.
 Summary: Knowing that his talkative wife will reveal to the world
that he has found a fortune buried on their farm, John arranges an
elaborate scheme to ensure that she will not be believed.
 ISBN 0-690-04809-2. — ISBN 0-690-04811-4 (lib. bdg.)
 ISBN 0-06-443292-0 (pbk.)
 [1. Behavior—Fiction. 2. Buried treasure—Fiction.] I. Duke,
Kate, ill. II. Title.
PZ7.C67346Don 1990   89-29283
[E]—dc20   CIP
                                                                  AC

First Harper Trophy edition, 1992.

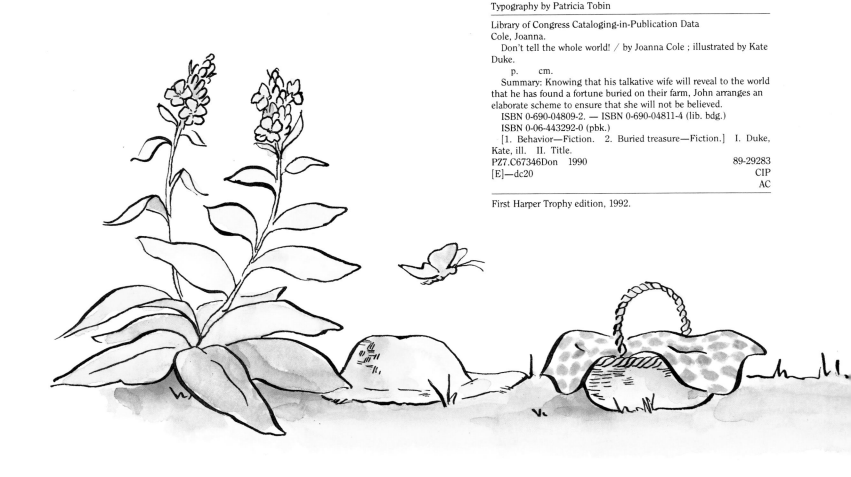

To Claire Schumacher

Once there was a woman who could not keep a secret.
It drove her husband crazy!

Suppose he had underwear with flowers on it....

Emma would see a bouquet at the
market and exclaim, "Look at those
flowers! They're just like the ones
on John's underwear!"

"You don't have to tell the whole
world!" John would say, all red and
frowning.

Then Emma would clap her hand over her mouth, too late.

"Next time, I won't tell," she'd promise.

And John couldn't stay mad at her. For he loved her dearly—even though he knew that, sooner or later, she would always tell every secret, no matter how big or how small. That is just the way she was.

Were they rich? No! They had no luck with money at all.

Every month when the rent was due on their farm, the rich landlord, Old Mr. Snood, came by. He didn't say "Hello." He didn't say "How are you?" He just said, "Where's the rent?"

One time Emma and John just didn't have the money.

"You'd better have it next week," growled Snood, "or I'll take your ox as payment."

The next day John was worried as he harnessed the ox to the plow.

"We'd better get some luck, old friend, or we'll soon be parted," said John.

The ox didn't worry. It just plowed the field as it always did. Then, all of a sudden, the plow hit something. *Clunk!*

It was a money box. And it must have been more than a hundred years old. There was enough money in that box to pay the rent for the rest of their lives!

What a stroke of luck! Right there in the field, John danced for joy. He expected the ox to be happy too, but the ox looked solemn.

"Oh, I get it," said John. "You're thinking of Emma."

The ox wouldn't say, one way or the other.

"She'll promise not to tell," continued John.

A gnat flew around the ox's nose, and the ox snorted.

"You're right," said John. "She'll tell anyway. And sooner or later Snood will find out. And will he let me keep the money?" The gnat flew into the ox's ear, and the ox shook its head.

"No, sir, he won't," agreed John. "He'll say that since the money was on his land, it belongs to him, even if it *has* been buried here for a hundred years. Well, I'm not going to let Snood get it.

14

"Good luck *visits* a lot of people," John continued,
"but it only *stays* with the ones who use their brains!"
So John sat down and used *his* brain. After a while,
he thought of a plan. He opened the box, put a few
coins in his pocket, and hid the rest. Then he tied the
ox in a shady spot and said, "Now I'm off to the market."

Later in the morning, John was back with the things he had bought. He hung a smoked fish in the branches of a tree.

He hid a jug of cider in a big old yellow weed.

And he scattered some hard brown molasses candies in the grass.

At noon, Emma came out to the field with his lunch.

"Not cabbage again," said John, acting disappointed. "I was hoping for a nice smoked fish."

"Where would I get a fish in the middle of a field?" asked Emma.

"There's one in that tree," said John.

"Are you crazy?" said Emma. "Fish don't grow on trees!"

"Watch this," said John, and he threw a rock up into the tree. A great big smoked fish fell down next to Emma.

Emma was so surprised, she couldn't say a word.

"Some cider would taste good with that fish," said John.

"All I brought is water," answered Emma.

"There's a cider jug growing over there," said John.

"You *are* crazy!" cried Emma.

"Go and look," said John.

Emma parted the leaves of the weed and pulled out a jug of the finest apple cider.

She was so surprised that she almost dropped it.

"Now, we need something sweet," said John. "This stone looks good."

He picked up a candy, brushed it off, and put it in his mouth.

"Stop!" shouted Emma. "You can't eat stones!"

"Try one," said John, and he popped a candy into her open mouth.

"It's delicious!" she said in amazement.

John almost laughed. But he was careful not to.

John and Emma sat down on the soft grass and ate their lunch. After a while, John got out the box.

"Open that up and see what's in it," he said.

Emma lifted the lid. The money shone up at her.

That was the most amazing thing of all. "Where did this come from?" she cried.

"I dug it up in the field," said John. "But it's a secret. Don't tell the whole world."

"I won't," she promised.

John ate some more of the "stones" and kept on smiling.

On the first day, Emma didn't tell anyone. On the second day, she almost told, but she held her tongue. On the third day, her neighbor came over.

"We can't pay the rent and Snood is going to throw us out of our house," wailed the neighbor.

Emma's good heart went out to her friend. "Don't worry," she blurted out. "With the money John found in the field, we'll help you out."

Well, the neighbor told her husband, and her husband told a man, and that man told another, and on market day Old Snood found out about it.

Snood went to see John. He didn't say "Hello." He didn't say "How are you?" He just said, "I hear you found money in my field. Hand it over!"

"What money . . . ?" John began. Then he laughed. "Oh, *that* money. That was just a dream my wife had."

"A dream, huh?" said Snood. He didn't believe it.

Snood went around to the house to ask Emma. This time he pretended to be friendly.

"Hello," he said. That was good luck you had, finding that money in my field."

"That wasn't the only luck we had that day!" said Emma.

"Really? There was more?" asked Snood, licking his lips with greed.

"John caught a fish in a tree, too," said Emma.

"A fish in a tree?" said Snood doubtfully.

"Oh, it was the most wonderful day. We drank the cider growing in a weed out there," said Emma.

"Cider in a weed?" echoed Snood.

"And the ground was all covered with sweet stones you can eat!" said Emma.

Snood didn't say "Good-bye." He didn't say "Thanks for the talk." He just stomped off.

"Money in the ground, fish in a tree, cider in a weed, stones you can eat!" he muttered to himself. "So it *was* a dream, after all!"

When Snood was gone, Emma told John what had happened.

"I thought Snood might try to get the money for himself," she said. "But he didn't even ask for it! Now we'll never have to worry about the rent again."

And she went inside, singing to herself.

As John put the ox in its stall, he whispered in its ear, "See what luck and brains can do together?" The ox nodded its head as it fell asleep.

Then John went into the house and kissed Emma
tenderly. For he loved her dearly, even though he
knew that she would always tell every secret, no
matter how big or how small.